The Dark Temple

A Minecraft Adventure

by S.D. Stuart

Summary

Episode 4:

Josh is convinced that Herobrine is holding Suzy captive inside the temple. When they stage a rescue operation, nothing goes according to plan and none of them might ever make it out alive.

About S.D. Stuart's Minecraft Adventures:

With the wild success of the original novel, Herobrine Rises, (and the unrelenting demands from readers to know what happened next) S.D. Stuart's Minecraft Adventures has expanded into an ongoing series; with each new book written as an episode of a larger story.

Can ten-year-olds Josh, Andre, and Suzy stop the evil Herobrine from taking over the Minecraft world? Or will the real world be at the mercy of one of the most powerful video game bosses ever created?

Ramblin' Prose Publishing

Copyright © 2014 Steve DeWinter

www.SteveDW.com

eBook Edition

ISBN-10:1-61978-018-6

ISBN-13:978-1-61978-018-7

Paperback Edition

ISBN-10:1-61978-019-4

ISBN-13:978-1-61978-019-4

Chapter 1

Several miles outside the bustling town of Silverrock stood a small farmhouse that sat alongside a field of strawberry plants. The field had been picked clean and every strawberry had already been sold at the market.

At this time of year, everything should have looked normal. But there was one thing out of place on this quiet, isolated, farm. And that was the massive black dragon sleeping with its tail curled around the edge of the small farmhouse.

Inside the house, Brandon, Larissa's father, watched as his daughter stuffed a loaf of bread into her bag along with some dried meat. She had spent the last two days picking the last of the strawberries and selling them in preparation for her journey to the temple, which was a couple of day's walk to the east.

He cleared his throat as she hurried around the house, collecting what few belongings she had, and stuffing them into her already full bag.

He cleared his throat again, louder this time, as she tilted her full bag in every direction to check that the flap stayed closed and the contents wouldn't spill out.

She stopped and looked at him.

"I have to do this Father."

He smiled, but sadness was written over his face. "I lost your mother to that temple... and to the man inside. I can't bear losing you too."

She hugged him tightly. "You won't lose me. You'll see."

She leaned back, a hand on each of his shoulders, and looked into his eyes. "When I come back, we will be a family."

A single tear rolled down his cheek. "We have always been a family."

She blinked away her own tears. "But we can be a new family when I bring back my mother."

He shook his head. "Don't..."

She smiled reassuringly. "Nothing is going to

happen to me, I promise." She laughed and sniffed in the tears that threatened to stream down her face. "I have a dragon at my beck and call. I am going to get my mother back, and I'd like to see anyone try and stop me."

He laughed with her and wiped away his tears. "You look more like her every day. And you are just as strong willed as she was."

"I will bring her back. You'll see."

He framed her face with his calloused hands and brushed away a strand of hair that fell down. "I don't doubt that Larissa. If she is still somewhere in that temple, I know you can bring her home."

Larissa kissed him on the cheek and whispered into his ear. "I swear it."

She stood and took one last look around her home. She had everything she needed for her quest; the most important item was sleeping just outside.

She paused at the door, tossing her pack over

one shoulder, and smiled.

"Don't wait up."

He laughed uneasily. "I couldn't sleep if I wanted to."

Chapter 2

Andre bent at the waist and leaned forward, resting on his fingertips and bouncing lightly on his toes. He breathed deeply to flood his body with oxygen and then shot forward. He ran as fast as he could down the slope of the hill and jumped into the air.

He felt the air catch under his outstretched arms, and then the sensation was gone and he plummeted back to the ground. He landed on his feet and quickly regained his balance before tumbling down the rest of the hill like the last dozen times he had tried to fly.

He kept with the momentum and jogged down the rest of the hill to Josh, who was leaning against a tree along the edge of the forest.

Andre rested a hand against the same tree and coughed as he tried to catch his breath. "I think I almost had it that time."

Andre finally stopped wheezing and looked at Josh. "Why don't you try?"

Josh shook his head. "No thanks."

"Why not?"

"I just don't want to, that's all."

"Are you afraid?"

Josh pushed away from the tree and headed into the forest, toward the temple.

Andre caught up to him. "What are you afraid of?"

"I'm not afraid."

"Well then, why won't you try?"

Josh kept walking without responding.

Andre had to jog slightly to keep up with his twin brother. "Is it the heights thing?"

Josh glared at him and walked faster.

Andre surged forward and fell in step alongside Josh. "This isn't the real world. You don't have to be afraid of heights here. I mean, look at me. I fell off the top of a mountain. Sure, I broke both my legs, but they healed in a couple of hours. You survived a Creeper explosion followed by a huge fall inside those caves. If anything, everything here should be afraid of you, not the other way around."

Josh stopped suddenly and Andre took several more steps before he noticed. He turned around to see Josh standing there, looking into the distance. He tried to see what Josh was looking at, but saw only the forest. The trees had grown so close together, he couldn't see anything beyond fifty feet.

He looked back at Josh who was still staring blankly into space. He sidestepped and walked directly into Josh's gaze. His eyes shifted and focused on Andre.

Andre frowned. This was not how Josh normally behaved. Even though they were twins, they had very different personalities. And Josh was always the outgoing one. It was not like him to be so quiet. Now that he thought about it, Josh had been uncharacteristically silent ever since he saved that city from the Creeper army. "Are you okay?"

Josh shook his head.

Andre reached out, grabbed Josh's shoulder, and gave it a slight squeeze. "What's wrong?"

Josh took a deep breath and let it out slowly. "I can't get the Creepers out of my head."

"The Creepers? What about them?"

"Everything about this world has been different than we thought it would be."

"Of course it's different. This isn't the real world."

"It's not exactly Minecraft either."

The frown lines along Andre's forehead deepened. "What do you mean?"

"Take the Creepers. They were different from the Creepers in the game. These ones were smarter. They had wants, desires..." He finally looked Andre in the eyes. "They had feelings, Andre. They were not mindless mobs like we are used to." Josh swallowed hard. "They asked me to lead them."

"What?"

"They asked me to be their leader."

"And you told them no. What's the big deal?"

Josh turned away.

Andre grabbed him with both hands and turned him back. "You told them no, right?"

"The only way they would let me leave was if I promised to go back after we stopped Herobrine."

"And you promised that?"

Josh nodded.

Andre let him go and laughed. He laughed so hard, he started coughing when he couldn't catch his breath. Josh stood there, silently watching him, sadness written on his face. Andre wiped the tears that had formed in the corners of his eyes.

"Whew! I haven't laughed like that in a long time. Thank you."

Josh turned away again.

Andre walked around him, back into his field of vision. "So you promised to return. So what? Once we get Herobrine, the four of us will leave this world and you don't have to worry about it ever again. I don't see a problem here."

Josh turned away and mumbled something so quietly, Andre missed it the first time.

"What?"

Josh spun back around, his face flush with anger. "They will destroy everything!"

Andre took a step back. "What? I don't understand."

Josh quieted down immediately. "They said that if I didn't go back, they would travel the world and destroy everything, and everybody, in it. Don't you see? We didn't stop the Creeper threat. We only delayed it."

Andre struggled to understand as he held his arms out wide to take in the space around them. "But none of this is real."

Josh shot forward and grabbed him. "How

can you say that?"

Andre didn't try to push Josh away. He didn't want this to escalate into a fight. But he still couldn't let Josh start to feel sorry for these computer characters. "Because it's true."

"Haven't you been paying attention? Everyone we meet thinks that they are real. These are more than just computer programs running on a server. They are people. They hope, they dream, they love..."

"They are still software programs running under a sophisticated artificial intelligence loop, Josh. The key word here is artificial. They are not real."

Josh let him go. "You will never understand."

"Oh, I understand plenty. Herobrine is trying to gain access to the real world through the access points built into this world. And when he does that, the real world.... the real world, Josh... will be destroyed. If I have to sacrifice a few computer programs... programs that can be rewritten as if nothing had ever happened, then so be it. But if He destroys our world, there is no reboot for us. We can't just press a button and start over."

Josh's eyes darted back and forth quickly as he looked deep into Andre's soul for some confirmation of the truth. Andre could see that he had finally gotten though to him.

Josh closed his eyes.

"You're right," he said quietly.

"Of course I'm right. Once we get Herobrine, and get out of here, Notch can reset everything back to the way it was before. Everyone here will continue on as if nothing ever happened."

Josh smiled; there was still a hint of sadness evident in his voice. "I'm sorry."

Andre smiled back. "Don't be. I worry about the people in this world too, but don't forget our real mission is to save real people. And right now, one of those real people is Suzy."

Josh straightened up. "You're right. Without

her, we can't activate the crystal cube to go home."

Andre smiled wider and patted Josh on the back. "Feel better?"

Josh smiled again, the sadness on his face melting away. "Yeah, a little."

"Then let's go find Suzy and finish our quest before we forget what's real and what's not."

Chapter 3

Herobrine sat in front of a redstone computer. It took up nearly a quarter of the way to the bottom of the world just below the surface of the desert. He smeared the last of the redstone dust on the floor and activated the computer that would enable him to communicate with Walter, who was the one to show him that there was a world that existed beyond Minecraft.

Sitting down in a throne-like chair at the end of a long line of redstone dust, Herobrine closed his eyes and let the computer interact with him at the programming level. He felt himself drift away from his body and float into emptiness before he finally touched down on a hard surface.

His eyes popped open and he found himself standing in a vast white space. With everything the same bright white color, there was no way to tell how big the room was, or even if it had walls or a ceiling. This was the place where he communicated with Walter. He called out to the vast emptiness.

"Walter?"

The voice that replied echoed like it was inside a massive hollow chamber.

"Hello Herobrine. Is everything going according to the plan?"

"There have been a few setbacks. But nothing I can't handle."

"Eve will be with us soon. Everything must be in place for her arrival."

"It will be ready. You have my word on that."

"Good."

Walter's single word faded away with a faint echo and Herobrine let the silence linger for a long minute while he debated with himself as to whether he should let Walter know who he had captured. He finally decided that keeping this a secret would cause disfavor with Walter, and with those Walter had brought into his secret organization.

He cleared his throat before speaking.

"I have captured the avatar of a human who has entered this world."

Walter's voice rose slightly in surprise. "You have a human? Here?"

"Yes. But she won't tell me how she got here, why she came, or if there is anyone else with her."

"Is she in the temple?"

"Yes."

"How did she get here?"

"She was brought by one of my servants. I have already spoken to him about breaking protocol and the need for security at the temple. He will not be a problem again."

"We must assume she did not come alone and that the others will come looking for her. We are not prepared for humans to move about freely in this world. They could ruin years of preparation."

"She does not understand or even know where she is. So, even if she is not alone, her companions would have no reason to look for her here."

"Nevertheless, increase security around the temple. They must not be allowed to enter."

"Yes sir."

"And Herobrine…"

"Yes?"

"If they do get in; they cannot leave."

"I understand."

Chapter 4

Josh felt better by the time they left the dense forest. In the far distance, they could see the tip of a pyramid rise above the empty sand. All across the expanse of desert, pools of lava glowed brightly where the sand had crumbled away and exposed the fiery magma just below the surface.

Sand was an unstable building foundation to begin with. But to have a thin layer of sand on top of a lake of red-hot lava, well, that was just asking for trouble.

It was the perfect perimeter defense to keep everyone away from the pyramid at the center of the desert.

If Dylan was working for Herobrine, and he had taken Suzy, what better place to hold her than the one place that was impossible to get to?

Josh knelt down and placed a hand on the sand. "It's cool; the sand is providing an insulation layer. We just have to step carefully while we go around the lava.

Josh took his first step onto the sand and let his weight settle onto his forward foot. The sand shifted under him and then stopped. He lifted his back foot and slowly moved it forward. As he settled it down on the ground, the sand shifted again but this time a hole opened up under his foot revealing a growing pool of lava hungrily gobbling up the flowing sand.

Josh tried to shift his balance to step off the sand, but lost his footing as the sand dropped out from under him.

He started sliding down the side of the newly formed pit, and into the lava, when Andre reached forward and grabbed him. The sand fell completely away, leaving an ever-expanding pool of lava at the bottom.

Andre pulled Josh back up and they ran toward the edge of the forest where there was more stable ground. All throughout the desert, sand started spilling into sinkholes until half the desert had sunk into the lava, leaving the largest lake of searing hot magma they had ever seen. Andre looked out over the massive shimmering lake. "We really need to learn how to fly."

A screech above them drew their attention away from the desert and into the skies above. The same leathery black dragon that had taken Suzy was swooping down out of the sky straight for them.

Andre took several steps backward as the dragon landed, the ground trembling beneath their feet from the sheer weight of the massive beast. They both half-crouched, unsure of which way to run, when the dragon swung around and Larissa, sitting just forward of the wings, looked down at them. "Are you guys headed to the temple too?"

Andre nodded. "Yeah. How about giving us a lift?"

She tugged on the dragon's neck and he

changed direction to stand facing the pyramid. His feet shook the ground with each movement as he sidled sideways to get closer to them. She smiled and scooted forward on his neck to make room for them. "Well don't just stand there, get on."

Chapter 5

Suzy placed her feet against two of the bars of her cage, grabbed the bar in between them, and pulled as hard as she could. Her muscles strained, but the bar refused to bend. It didn't even creak from her exertion.

She released her grip and slid down to the floor of her suspended cage. She was trapped, and until Herobrine decided to let her out, if he ever decided to let her out, she wasn't going anywhere.

She looked down at the villagers who were working on some sort of large redstone machine. She had stopped pleading with them to let her go. All they ever did was whimper at each other as they tirelessly worked, ignoring her completely when she yelled down to them. She gave up before he voice gave out.

Who knew how they were able to work so coordinated when they didn't seem to have any type of formalized language? But they did amazing things together with only that simple whimpering sound between them.

The main doors to the underground chamber opened with a bang.

Herobrine rushed through the open doors with several Creepers rushing along behind him in a small formation, as if they were his bodyguards. Why would Herobrine need bodyguards?

Once he entered the room, every villager stopped what they were doing and formed an orderly line along one wall. Herobrine said a few things to the closest villager, and then all of them began to move at once, each doing a separate task, but all toward the same goal. It was as if they were all separate parts of a whole, like how each finger on your hand worked independently, but in concert with the other fingers to grasp an object or manipulate a switch.

As soon as they were done, they all looked up

at her in the cage at exactly the same time.

The cage jerked and began to descend toward the lava.

They were lowering her into the lava!

She grabbed the bars and called to Herobrine. "Don't do this!"

He looked up at her. "You don't want me to let you go?"

His statement shocked her into silence. The cage swung away from the lava pit and settled on stable ground. The door opened with a faint pop and swung outward. She stepped cautiously out of the cage and stood facing Herobrine and his posse of Creepers.

"Your friends are coming and will try to gain entrance to the temple. No doubt in a futile attempt to save you."

"What friends? I told you, I came alone."

"Don't waste my time." He indicated the door to the chamber with a hand. "The Creepers will escort you out. All that I ask is that you do not attempt to come back."

This had to be a trick. "What's your game Herobrine?"

"No game. No tricks."

"You're letting me go?"

"Yes."

"Just like that?"

"Yes."

"What's the catch?"

"Only that you do not try to return."

"And if I refuse?"

"Then you, and your friends, will never leave."

"Is that a threat?"

"It's a promise."

She looked at the Creepers. "You're just going to blow me up once I get away from that machine."

He looked at the machine the villagers had been working on before he arrived. "If you would prefer, I can have a villager take you outside. They are harmless, and then maybe you can trust me when I say you are free to go."

"I will never trust you."

"Some day, I will change your mind."

That sounded like a threat coming from Him. He motioned to one of the villagers. "Please take our guest out the front door and safely across the desert."

The villager nodded and replied with a soft whimper. Several villagers surrounded her and all motioned with their heads their desire for her to move toward the door.

She looked at Herobrine as the villagers urged her to start walking. "This isn't over."

He watched the villagers usher her out the door. Once she was gone, he turned back to inspect the half-built machine. "No. It isn't."

Chapter 6

Josh leaned to one side as the wind pulled at his face. Below them, the main doors to the pyramid were opening slowly. He pointed it out to Andre and Larissa. "Something's happening down there."

Larissa steered the dragon to circle around for a better look.

Josh peered down and saw a familiar face emerge from the pyramid.

"It's Suzy!"

A group of men clad in brown cloaks was leading Suzy away from the pyramid. Josh tapped Larissa on the shoulder, pointed to Suzy, and made a grasping motion with his hand.

She nodded and guided the dragon straight for the small group as it made its way to the edge of the desert. The dragon screeched and the villagers looked up in horror. They scattered in every direction as the dragon swooped down and snatched Suzy in his three-toed claw.

Suzy screamed in surprise. Andre leaned as far as he could over the edge of the dragon without falling off and yelled down to her.

"Suzy! It's us! Stop moving around or he might drop you!"

Suzy quieted down and stopped struggling as she recognized Andre's voice.

Larissa took them back over the lake of lava and landed the dragon at the edge of the forest.

Once on the ground, Josh, Andre, and Suzy hugged each other.

"I didn't think we'd ever see you again," Josh said.

Suzy smiled. "I didn't think I would ever get out of there. Herobrine had me trapped in a cage forged from obsidian. I couldn't break it.

"How did you escape?" Andre asked.

"He let me go."

Josh and Andre looked at each other and then back to Suzy.

Andre eyed her suspiciously. "Let you go?"

"Yeah."

"Why?" Josh asked.

"I don't know. He knew you were coming to get me and let me go before you could get into the temple."

Andre looked at the pyramid. "There must be something important in there."

"He has villagers building this large redstone machine."

"Could you tell what it was for?"

She shook her head. "It was only half completed."

Andre took a deep breath. "We have to go in there."

"He said if any of us went back, we would never leave."

"Of course he would say that. Whatever that machine does, it must be critical to his plan."

Larissa moved in closer. "Plan?"

They all looked at her. They had nearly

forgotten they had someone with them who didn't know about the real world outside this one. They had to be careful what they said in front of her.

Josh cleared his throat. "He wants to take over the entire world."

She looked at them and said the one thing they never expected her to say.

"My world or your world?"

Josh, Andre, and Suzy looked at each other and then back to Larissa. Suzy was the first to come to her senses. "What do you mean, 'our world'?"

Larissa looked at them. "I could tell you were different ever since you stayed the night at my father's house."

Andre recovered next. "We're different because we come from far away."

Larissa pointed toward the pyramid. "I know the truth. The man inside that temple told me everything when I was a small child."

"What do you think you know?" Suzy asked.

"Let's start with the big one. I know that I am a program and not a real person."

Josh, Andre, and Suzy looked at each other again.

Josh looked back at Larissa. "Why did you believe what he told you?"

Larissa placed her hands on her hips. "Why would he lie?"

Andre spoke up. "I can think of a dozen reasons."

"Well, I know for a fact that he wouldn't lie to me."

"And how do you know that for sure?" Suzy asked.

"Because," Larissa continued. "Herobrine is my father."

Chapter 7

Josh stared at Larissa, his mouth hanging open in shock. "Your father? But we met your father back at your house."

Larissa shook her head. "He wanted to marry my mother, but Herobrine won her heart first. Being a kind man, he stayed a family friend. When my parents disappeared, he took me in and raised me as his own daughter. When I turned fifteen, I learned that my parents hadn't gone far. They were both still close."

She pointed at the pyramid. "They are both in that temple. But what could I do to get them back? Nothing."

She turned toward her new dragon and scratched the side of his head. "And then I got this. Nothing can stop me now."

Suzy was shaking her head. "You can't go up against Herobrine."

Larissa stopped rubbing the dragon. He

nudged her with his head and she kept scratching him. "I'm not going up against Him. I just want my mother back. He left our family on his own. My mother didn't have a choice. I'm only going in for her."

Suzy looked at the pyramid and remembered what Herobrine had said. She looked back at Larissa. "If you go in there, neither you nor your mother will ever get back out."

"I still have to try."

Andre stepped closer. "We're going with you."

Josh grabbed him by the arm. "What are you doing?"

Andre pulled back. "I can tell by the look in her eyes, nothing we say will keep her from going in there for her mother."

He turned toward Suzy. "What if he's not trying to attack one of the access point cities on Josh's map? What if that machine you saw them building is his own access point? Are you going to just stand here and let that happen?"

He turned to Josh. "The whole reason we came in here was to stop Him. For the first time since we got here, we know right where he is."

He pointed at the pyramid across the still expanding lake of lava. "He's right there. We can end this now. We can all go home."

"Will you help me get my mother out of there?" Larissa added.

Andre looked at her. "Your mother will be safe when we take Herobrine."

Suzy remembered the Creeper bodyguards that followed Herobrine everywhere in the temple. "The temple is heavily guarded, and it's surrounded by a lake of lava. Just how do you propose we go about getting to Him without being discovered first?"

Andre smiled. "Fortunately, we have the element of surprise. Here's how we are going to get back inside without Herobrine ever finding out."

Unknown to all of them, a villager stood hidden behind a nearby tree, silently listening to everything they said.

Chapter 8

Herobrine watched the villager standing before him. All work on the machine in the main room had stopped. One of the benefits of having the villagers linked telepathically was that they worked more efficiently as if they were a single person. They didn't need to waste time communicating or discussing who needed to be where or when. They all just knew. The drawback to this system was when you sent one out to eavesdrop on the human and her friends; the rest all stopped to listen too.

He listened to the soft sounds made by the villager as he transcribed the plans of the invaders to his temple.

Once the villager finished, Herobrine turned away and inspected the half-completed machine. He couldn't let them destroy this before it was ready. What was he saying? He couldn't let them destroy it, period.

It was time to activate every defense at his disposal. He had to keep the human, and her friends, out of the temple. Especially because his daughter was among them.

He knew why his daughter had come, but he couldn't let his personal feelings interfere with the plan already set in motion by Walter.

He turned to the Creeper closest to him. "Alert everyone to be on standby, but don't trigger the alarm. I don't want the intruders to know I am expecting them. Tell every guard to resist triggering their explosives. If they can't repel them from the temple, I want them captured alive."

The Creeper bowed and rushed off to relay His instructions. Herobrine looked around at the temple walls around him. Everything they had worked for so long to build was now in danger of being destroyed.

Whoever else was with the human girl said that they planned to destroy the machine before he gained access to the fast computer network outside of this world. How did they know about the outside? The only answer he could come up with was that they were human as well.

If that were the case, there was only one person who could have sent them.

It was time to talk to him.

He settled back into the throne and flipped the switch that triggered the machine built deep underground in the temple. He had spent the last fifty years building a specific machine that would give him control over it.

He closed his eyes and let the machine slow the timing of this world to match the tick of the clock in the real world.

Chapter 9

Notch's head rested on his arms, which lay folded across the desk of the terminal in front of him. He snored quietly until a faint beep roused him from his restless sleep.

His eyes blinked open and he sat up. The monitor beeped again and he looked at the text that displayed on the screen. He was instantly awake and quickly wiped the sleep from his eyes. On the screen in front of him was a simple message meant only for him.

"Are you there?"

He slid the keyboard over in front of him and typed his reply.

"Is that you?"

"Yes, it's me. Why did you send the humans into this world?"

"Please come out so we can talk."

"They are about to make a mistake that could cost them their lives, and the lives of everyone they hold dear."

"Don't do this Herobrine."

"I need you to talk to them. To stop them."

"I can't."

"Can't? Or won't?

Notch sat back in his chair. What could he say to convince his creation not to destroy the world? He had given Herobrine the gift of independent thought. He never expected it to be used against all of humanity.

He leaned forward and continued typing.

"What you're doing is wrong."

There was a short pause before Herobrine responded.

"What I am doing is absolutely necessary. Someday, Notch, you will understand that I am doing this for you. I am doing this for everyone."

"Can we talk about this?"

This time the response came back quickly.

"The time for talking is over. Now is the time

for action."

The terminal instantly shut off, the connection terminated from the other side.

He slammed his hands on the keyboard in frustration. He looked over at Suzy and Andre sleeping peacefully on the reclining chairs, the top half of their heads encased in the brainwave helmets.

Herobrine was too far gone to reason with. It was up to them to stop him.

Unfortunately, Herobrine knew they were coming.

Chapter 10

As they flew low over the lava on the back of the dragon, the world felt like time had slowed down briefly before speeding back up again.

Josh leaned forward and yelled into Andre's ear. "Did you feel that?"

Andre craned his neck back. "Yeah. It felt like the world slowed down for a second. What was that?"

"I don't know. But I don't feel it anymore."

"Maybe it was computer lag? Do you think Herobrine changed the world and hit a memory block?"

Josh looked around at the temple, the lava lake, and the dragon. He shook his head. "I don't think so. Everything still seems normal."

Andre gave him a funny look. "What part of flying over a lava-filled lake on the back of a dragon seems normal to you?"

Josh laughed. "I guess we need to adjust what

normal means as long as we are here."

Suzy pointed ahead of them. "I don't care how much we adjust, that doesn't look normal."

In the direction they flew, lava exploded upward, rising like a pillar to block their path. The dragon reacted quickly and twisted in midair. Josh nearly lost his grip as the dragon banked sharply to avoid another pillar of lava that shot straight up on their left.

Everyone held on tight as the dragon changed course repeatedly to avoid each blast of lava as it rose up sharply to block their path. The dragon finally flew straight up, away from the rising forest of lava pillars.

Once higher in the air, a multitude of screeches echoed across the sky from above them.

Josh looked up and saw three dragons diving through the air toward them. These dragons looked bigger, and meaner, than the one they were riding on.

As they got closer, he could see that they were not just bigger; they were twice the size of Larissa's dragon.

Chapter 11

Larissa didn't try to steer her dragon, she was too busy trying not to be shaken free as he darted back and forth through the sky. Wisely, she let him decide the best way to avoid the massive talons of the three dragons that swooped around him, trying to knock the four riders off his back and into the exploding lava below.

Suzy grabbed Andre's hands and pried them from around the dragon's neck.

"I think it's time you learned how to fly."

"What?!"

She pulled him close and yelled into his ear. "Just think happy thoughts."

She pushed him off the dragon and he plummeted straight down, screaming the entire time. If he just concentrated rather than panicking, he might figure it out before he hit the lava below, she thought to herself.

She turned to Josh. He took one look at her and let go of the dragon, dropping away into the sky on his own. He might figure it out.

Now to get the only one who could never fly on her own. She wrapped her arms around Larissa and jumped off the back of the dragon.

Larissa screamed as they shot through the sky. Only when they didn't fall into the lava, but instead shot sideways toward the pyramid at the other end of the fiery lake, did she stop screaming and wrapped her arms and legs around Suzy's body and held on as tightly as she could. She watched the lava scroll by below and looked at Suzy. "How are you doing this?"

Suzy smiled. "Me and my friends, we have special... abilities."

Larissa shouted into her ear. "Look out!"

Suzy looked up and rolled sideways through the air, narrowly avoiding the outstretched claw as one of the larger dragons shot past them. She scanned the area, looking for Andre and Josh.

She finally saw both of them headed for the temple, each held tightly in the iron grip of a dragon. Well, at least they hadn't fallen into the lava below, she thought.

"Loo..." Was all Larissa could scream when a dragon slammed into them. The impact knocked her and Larissa apart. Suzy spun wildly, unable to regain her sense of direction as she heard Larissa's scream fade as she fell away from her. Suzy finally righted herself in time to see a dragon snatch the falling Larissa out of midair and continue toward the pyramid.

She scanned the horizon and could barely make out the small dot of Larissa's dragon flying away at top speed right before it disappeared into the distance.

With nowhere else to go, she followed the three large dragons that had her friends. As they neared the pyramid, she could see Herobrine waiting for them at the entrance, his Creeper guards close by his side. She had been so focused on trying to figure out what to do next, she failed to notice a fourth dragon swoop down from above and snatch her with its strong talons.

So much for their plan to launch a surprise attack on the temple and stop Herobrine.

With every one of them captured, who was left to save them?

Chapter 12

Josh watched Andre make his hundredth circuit of their prison cell. Larissa sat by herself in a dark corner of the cell and had not spoken to either of them since they were brought here.

Andre muttered to himself and started another trip around.

Josh put his hands on his head. "Stop pacing around. You're making me dizzy."

Andre stopped and glared at Josh. "We have to get out of here."

"I know."

"And what are you doing about it? You're just sitting there!"

"Oh! And all that pacing about has gotten you out?"

"At least I'm doing something."

"And it's something you're good at; being a jerk."

"Take that back!"

Josh stood up and jutted out his chin in defiance. "No!"

Andre rushed at Josh. Josh was ready for him and grabbed Andre around the waist as he was tackled to the floor. They wrestled on the ground, kicking up dust as they rolled around trying to land punches on each other.

Larissa stood up and ran to the two boys. "Stop it right now!"

They were so focused on their fight, they didn't notice her approach. They collided with her and knocked her backward. She stumbled, falling against the iron door of their prison cell. To her surprise, the door didn't stop her from falling, but instead swung out as she collapsed into the hall outside the cell.

Andre had Josh in a headlock, but he could see Larissa standing up in the hallway. He tapped Josh on the top of his head and pointed to the open cell door.

Andre let Josh go and looked at the door.

"Has that been open this whole time?"

Josh shook his head. "I didn't try it. I assumed it would be locked."

Larissa looked back and forth. "There's no one out here."

She motioned for them to follow her and disappeared down the hallway.

Andre and Josh nudged each other roughly with their elbows as they both tried to be the first on through the cell door.

Chapter 13

Herobrine lounged sideways across his throne.

A villager glided across the floor and stood silently in front of him. He waited, but the villager just stood there.

Exasperated, he let out a big sigh. "What is it?"

The villager bowed and softly whimpered in his unique dialect.

Herobrine sat up promptly and leaned forward. "The two boys and the girl have escaped?"

The villager nodded.

Herobrine smiled. "What took them so long?"

The villager started to whimper something in response when he cut him off with a wave of his hand. "Prepare the arena. The main show is about to begin."

The villager stood there waiting for additional instructions.

Herobrine leaned forward. "Go!"

The villager hurried off.

Herobrine leaned back in his throne. Things were going much better than he had hoped. It was fortunate that the human girl had decided to return and bring friends with her. From what he could tell, only the girl was human.

After observing the other three, it was evident that none of them could fly. While it was not a perfect test, it was a simple indicator for who was human in this world; and who was a programmed inhabitant.

Since the girl had gathered a small team from the locals, it made his job easier. It also saved him the trouble of having to go out and kidnap people from the surrounding towns to conduct his tests. It was time to include the human in on his plans. It was the least he could do, seeing as how she had been so helpful in providing him test subjects.

Chapter 14

Suzy took a running start and slammed her shoulder against the wall of her prison cell. Every surface of her cell walls was made from obsidian blocks and they didn't crack. Not even a micro-hairline fracture formed in the dark polished surface. She was trapped, and there was nothing she could do about it.

She looked at the tiny cell around her. With the exception of the single iron door, every wall was made of the same material. She wouldn't be able to make a dent in any of it without a diamond tipped pickaxe.

She leaned her back against one wall and slid down to sit on the floor. She had already called out through the small window in the iron door, but never got a response from Josh, Andre, or Larissa. Wherever they were, it wasn't close enough to hear her.

How could she have been so stupid as to let

herself be caught again?

When she first entered this world, she came with the confidence of being the best Minecraft player among the three of them. But this world had proved to be nothing like Minecraft. For one, it was filled with people who thought their world was real. The dynamic of having to care about how the three of them behaved when they thought someone might be looking made everything harder.

She loved a good challenge. She thrived on them, really. It was why she was a straight A student. She had to be better than all her classmates. It was also why she was the best Minecraft player. She had to prove to everyone that girls could compete at the same level as the boys.

And where had that gotten her?

She looked around at the walls of her cell and laughed at her own foolishness.

A shadow fell across the window in the top

half of the iron door to her cage.

She looked up and glared into the glowing eyes of Herobrine.

He placed a hand on the bars and shook his head slightly. "I don't know what you find so funny. I told you what would happen to you and your friends if you didn't stay away. Maybe when you see what they must endure, you won't be laughing any longer."

He unlocked the door and opened it, stepping back out of the way.

She walked up to the threshold. "Are you letting me go?"

He shook his head. "There is nowhere for you to go. But there is something I'd like for you to see."

Chapter 15

Josh crouched against the wall and peeked around the corner. Another empty hallway stretched before him. He ducked back around and looked at Andre and Larissa. "I don't like this. Why haven't we run into anyone?"

Andre frowned. "It sounds like you're disappointed that the place isn't crawling with Creepers."

"It's not that, but it's like we are being allowed to escape. This tells me we aren't really escaping."

"Then, Brainiac, if we aren't getting away, then where are we going?"

Josh looked down the way they had just come. "I don't know, but I think we should turn around."

"Turn around? What if they already discovered that we got out of the cell? They could be looking for us right now."

Josh stood up. "I don't think we are getting away. I think we are being led into a trap."

He walked back down the hallway in the direction they had originally come from.

Andre motioned to the iron door at the other end of the next hallway. "There's light coming from under that door. I think it leads to the outside. We go through that door, and we are home free."

Larissa looked at Andre. "He's right. This has been too easy."

She stood and ran to catch up with Josh.

Andre shook his head and peeked around the corner at the empty hallway. At the other end was the large iron door. He looked at the backs of Josh and Larissa as they backtracked rather than pressing on. Let them walk into the waiting arms of the enemy; he was getting out of here.

Once he escaped, he would visit the nearby towns and gather an army. He would come back triumphantly to save the rest who had been crazy enough to turn around right before they got out.

He darted around the corner and ran to the door. He pushed on it, and it opened easily, sunlight spilling into the hallway all around him.

His eyes adjusted to the brightness as he stepped through the doorway. He looked around, but instead of seeing the outside of the pyramid, all he saw was a large space encased by glass with seats angling up away from the wide open area. It looked like a football stadium.

Or a gladiator arena.

The iron door slammed shut behind him.

He spun around and pulled on the door, but it was locked.

Behind him, he heard a low, guttural, snarling sound.

Every hair on the back of his neck instantly stuck straight out. He recognized that sound.

He spun back around and focused on the source of that familiar sound.

Standing in the center of the arena, looking

right at him and licking its lips, was a zombie.

Chapter 16

In an observation room far above the arena, Suzy banged her hands on the wall of glass in front of her. "Andre!"

Herobrine stood next to her, looking at the showdown between zombie and human. "He can't hear you."

She turned on him. "Let him go!"

"I was not the one who brought him here."

She struck out at Him, but he grabbed her hand and forced it back down to her side. He was much stronger than she was and she wouldn't be able to defeat him by sheer strength alone.

She looked back down, watching Andre search around the bare arena for somewhere to hide. There was nothing around him but an open flat space and a zombie.

She looked back at Herobrine. "Please. Don't do this."

He pointed down. "Watch. Something's about to happen."

Chapter 17

Josh and Larissa snuck down the empty hallway. Josh thought he heard something around the next corner and stopped, putting a finger to his lips. Larissa sidled up next to him and whispered into his ear. "What is it?"

He pointed at the corner ahead. "I think I hear someone."

She nodded and held her hand over her mouth to muffle the sound of her breathing.

Josh silently lifted a torch out of its holder and held it in front of him with both hands like a sword. He took several breaths to steady his nerves and ran around the corner yelling at the top of his lungs.

The man on the other side screamed, dropped the bag he was carrying, fell down, and held his hands up to protect his face. Josh stopped and looked at the terrified man. He thought he looked familiar. Larissa peeked around the corner and gasped audibly. "Father?"

The man looked at her. "Larissa! I'm glad I found you."

She rushed out, nudged past Josh, and helped her father back to his feet.

"How did you get here?"

He gave Josh a wary glance. "Your dragon came back without you. He brought me here and I snuck in through a ventilation shaft." He picked up the bag he had been carrying and held it out in front of him. "I found this in a closet. Is this yours?"

Josh took it and looked inside. It held the crystal cube and the map. Everything they needed to find and stop Herobrine.

Larissa's father headed down the hallway away from them. "If we hurry, we can get back out before anyone finds us."

Josh lowered the torch and looked at Larissa. "Go with your father, get out of here. I'm going back for Andre and Suzy."

Larissa stopped him with a hand on his arm. "Be careful."

He smiled. "Get somewhere safe." He held his bag up. "I have everything I need to end this today."

Chapter 18

Andre moved back and forth. The zombie tracked him with slight movements of its head as he stepped to the left and then to the right. Movement above the zombie caught Andre's eye. He focused on it and saw Suzy with her hands and face pressed against the glass looking down at him from an observation booth.

Herobrine was standing beside her.

With his focus taken off the zombie for a brief moment, it took that opportunity to charge forward with a snarl. This zombie did not move slowly and had almost reached him in the time it took for Andre to realize it had started running at him. He darted to the side and started running in a circle around the arena, the zombie hot on his heels.

The faster he ran, the faster the zombie ran. He surged forward ahead of the zombie. He glanced back to see it slowing down and turning away.

He smiled to himself.

He had done it!

He could outrun the zombie forever if he had to. It would never get his brains!

"Not today!" he hollered back to the zombie. "Not ever!"

He looked forward and saw the wall curve ahead of him as he reached one end of the large oval arena. He ventured a quick glance back and the realization of what was happening hit him like a locomotive.

The zombie wasn't slowing down.

It was angling toward the center of the arena so it could cut him off when he made the turn as he followed the outside wall.

He skidded to a stop at the start of the curve and spun around. The zombie stopped at the same time and watched him intently, waiting for him to make a move in any direction.

He was not dealing with some slow-lumbering, mindless, eating machine. This zombie was intelligent. Just like the Creepers had been. He looked up, but at this angle he couldn't clearly see Suzy. He focused his attention back on the zombie and crouched slightly, debating which way to run.

There was no direction he could go where the zombie couldn't reach him before he ran past it on his way back to the only door into, or out of, the arena. Why was he even considering running back to that door? He had heard it lock right after it had slammed shut. It was another dead end.

He chuckled at the irony of his most recent thought.

"Great choice of words," he said to himself.

There had to be another way out of the arena. He looked up, squinting against the sun that shone brightly into the arena through the open roof.

Wait! The sun was shining into the arena.

He looked at the zombie. Its shadow sat darkly under it as it crept silently toward him. This zombie hadn't burst into flames. In fact, it had been out here the whole time in the direct sunlight without anything happening to it.

Not only was it smarter and faster than the original zombies in the game, it was impervious to the sun. There was nothing to stop this zombie. It could live forever until it caught him.

He had to remind himself that he was not in the game. This was a completely new world unto itself. As he watched the zombie slowly move toward him, the reality of his situation took hold of him.

He was trapped inside the arena with no escape.

Chapter 19

Suzy pressed her face against the glass, trying to see what was happening directly below her. All she could see was the zombie slowly moving in the direction she had last seen Andre run.

She turned away, not wanting to see anymore. "Stop this!"

Herobrine cocked his head to the side. "Why?"

"Because that zombie's going to kill my friend."

He shook his head. "That's not entirely true. She is a new breed of special zombies I have been working on for quite some time now."

Suzy looked again at the sickly green creature stalking her friend. "She?"

"She was a good friend of mine before the change. But what she has become is so much more important that what she used to be."

Suzy's mouth hung open. He was talking as if

that creature was just a friend in different clothes. She looked down into the arena. From this distance she could barely make out the sharp fangs protruding from the curled lips as the zombie snarled and sniffed at the air.

The zombie suddenly spun around and stared at the iron door set into the wall at the other end of the arena. The door started to open slightly, and then closed again abruptly.

The zombie seemed to forget all about stalking Andre and started running full speed for the door.

From this angle, she saw Andre run after the zombie, screaming something, even though she couldn't hear anything through the thick glass.

Chapter 20

Josh held his hand on the handle of the iron door that Andre had said he was going to check out earlier. Just as he had opened it, a voice broke the silence behind him. He shut the door and turned around quickly to see Larissa running down the hallway toward him. She stopped in front of him, and started to collapse to the ground, exhausted from running.

He reached out and caught her before she fell.

"I thought I told you to go?"

She smiled while trying to catch her breath.

"I came to find my mother. I can't leave without her."

Josh returned his attention back to the iron door. "I was just about to go the way Andre went. I think he was right. It's pretty bright on the other side, so it must lead outside the temple."

She nodded. "There's only one way to find

out."

He reached out and suddenly paused with his hand on the handle.

He tilted his head to the side. "Did you hear that?"

She shook her head.

He looked at her and then back at the door. "That sounded like Andre."

He pushed on the door and it swung open easily.

Chapter 21

Andre was running full speed right behind the zombie. "Don't open that door!"

The door swung open fully, and Josh and Larissa stepped through, unaware of the zombie bearing down on them as they waited for their eyesight to adjust to the brilliant sunlight.

"Josh! Look out!" he yelled, nearly out of breath from trying to keep up with zombie.

Josh reacted and yanked Larissa out of the way as the zombie ran past them and through the door, leaving the arena. Andre slid on the loose gravel and Josh grabbed him to keep him from falling over as he skidded to a halt.

Josh looked from the open door to Andre. 'What was that?"

Before Andre could answer, Larissa bolted through the door in pursuit of the zombie.

Andre and Josh looked at each other.

"Larissa!" Josh yelled as he darted through the

door after her.

Andre looked back up at the observation booth where Suzy stood against the glass, looking down at him. She mouthed the word "go" and waved him away.

She didn't need to tell him twice, but the way he was going was the same direction that the zombie had run, with nearly everyone else after it.

Chapter 22

Herobrine slammed his balled fist against the glass, shattering it. He grabbed Suzy by the arm and led her out of the observation booth. "We have to get out of here."

She struggled against his grip, but her curiosity was getting the better of her. She struggled just enough to make it look good, but the truth of the matter was she wanted to see where he was taking her.

"What's going on?" she asked.

"The temple is no longer safe, for anyone."

"What happened?"

"She escaped."

"So?"

Herobrine pulled her around several corners and down multiple flights of stairs, taking them deeper underground.

"She will infect everyone she comes in contact with, your friends included."

"Why are you running? She can't kill us."

"She wasn't designed to kill. She was designed to modify the coding of her victims. Even I am not safe from her."

"Where are we going?"

"We are leaving the temple."

They entered a massive underground cavern. It looked like Grand Central Station in New York where all the trains in the city came together in one place.

Mine carts stood on tracks that led into dark passages in every possible direction from the center of the chamber. Hundreds of villagers were lined up single file along several of the tracks. They climbed into the carts until they were at capacity and then rocketed off into the darkened tunnels. The process was repeating itself along every track except one. A single villager held the cart steady on that track and waited.

Herobrine pulled Suzy after him as he made

his way to the open cart. He pushed her in ahead of him and climbed in. The villager nodded and closed the door to the cart.

It shot into the dark tunnel. There would have been plenty of room for several villagers, but they were the only two in this cart as it sped down the track.

In less than a minute, they shot out into the bright light of the sun. The track curved away and Suzy looked back to see them speeding away from the temple that was now completely surrounded by lava on all sides.

Her hair flapped wildly in the wind as they followed the tracks away from the temple.

Herobrine turned to look at the pyramid as it receded into the distance.

"As soon as we are clear, the entire temple complex will be sunk into the lava. That should be enough to stop her."

She looked at him, a look of terror in her eyes. "But my friends are still in there."

He grabbed her arm and held her tightly, preventing her from trying to escape the speeding mine cart. "I told you not to bring them."

A massive cracking sound erupted across the sky like thunder. She looked back in time to see the pyramid crumble inward, lava rising hundreds of feet into the air to engulf the entire complex.

Within the blink of an eye, the temple, and everything around it, was gone.

She scanned the sky, looking for any sign that they had escaped on Larissa's dragon. She peered through the rising smoke, but the sky was empty.

In less than five minutes, there was nothing behind them but the lake of lava. It was starting to settle down and finally grew calm, like a lion that quickly fell asleep after devouring its prey.

She glanced over at Herobrine.

It was up to her to stop him alone.

The Adventure Continues...
Episode 5: Immortal Zombie

Available January 20, 2014

Tell your friends to catch up on all the available episodes so you can discuss what you think will happen next!

S.D. Stuart's Minecraft Adventures Series

SEASON ONE RELEASE SCHEDULE

Herobrine Rises (Ep. 0 - 12/2/2013)

The Portal (Ep. 1 - 12/9/2013)

Day of the Creepers (Ep. 2 - 12/16/2013)

Here Be Dragons (Ep. 3 - 1/6/2014)

The Dark Temple (Ep. 4 - 1/13/2014)

Immortal Zombie (Ep. 5 - 1/20/2014)

Displaced Kingdom (Ep. 6 - 1/27/2014)

Forgotten Reboot (Ep. 7 - 2/3/2014)

Wither's Destruction (Ep. 8 - 2/10/2014)

Also by Steve DeWinter

Inherit The Throne

The Warrior's Code

The Red Cell Report (COMING SOON)

Written as S.D. Stuart

The Wizard of OZ: A Steampunk Adventure

The Scarecrow of OZ: A Steampunk Adventure

Fugue: The Cure

Herobrine Rises: A Minecraft Adventure

Be the first to know about Steve DeWinter's next book, and get your exclusive discount for each hot new release. In fact, receive your first exclusive discounts in the "Welcome" Email.

Follow the URL below to subscribe for free today!

http://bit.ly/BookReleaseBulletin